The Magic School Bus
Lost in the Solar System

By Joanna Cole   Illustrated by Bruce Degen

SCHOLASTIC INC. / New York

The author and illustrator wish to thank
Dr. Donna L. Gresh,
Center for Radar Astronomy at Stanford University,
for her assistance in preparing this book.

The author also thanks John Stoke,
Astronomical Writer/Producer at the American Museum-Hayden Planetarium,
for his helpful advice.

Library of Congress Cataloging-in-Publication Data
Cole, Joanna.
The magic school bus, lost in the solar system.
Summary: On a special field trip in the magic school bus,
Ms. Frizzle's class goes into outer space and visits each planet
in the solar system.
1. Outer space — Exploration — Juvenile literature. 2. Astron-
omy — Juvenile literature. [1. Planets. 2. Solar System.
3. Astronomy.]
I. Degen, Bruce, ill. II. Title.
QB500.22.064   1990   523.3   89-10185
ISBN 0-590-41428-3

18 17 16 15 14 13 12   5 6 7 8 9/9

Printed in the U.S.A.   36

First printing, October 1990

To Virginia and Bob McBride—J.C.

For Chris, queen of the
Biscadorian Mother ship—B.D.

We tried to be nice to Janet.
We really did.
As we got on the school bus,
we told her that Ms. Frizzle
is the weirdest teacher in school.
But Janet wasn't interested.
She wanted to tell us about herself.

As usual, it took a while to get the old bus started.
But finally we were on our way.
As we were driving, Ms. Frizzle told us all about how the Earth spins like a top as it moves in its orbit.
It was just a short drive to the planetarium, but Ms. Frizzle talked fast.

THIS BUS IS A WRECK.

AT LEAST IT STARTED THIS TIME.

WE HAVE NEW SCHOOL BUSES AT OUR SCHOOL.

WHAT MAKES NIGHT AND DAY?
by Phoebe
The spinning of the Earth makes night and day.
When one side of the Earth faces the Sun it is daytime on that side. When that side turns away from the Sun, it is night.

WHEN THE EARTH SPINS WE SAY IT ROTATES. THE EARTH MAKES ONE COMPLETE ROTATION— TURN—EVERY 24 HOURS.

When we got to the planetarium,
it was closed for repairs.
"Class, this means we'll
have to return to school,"
said the Friz.
We were so disappointed!

On the way back,
as we were waiting at a red light,
something amazing happened.
The bus started tilting back,
and we heard the roar of rockets.
"Oh, dear," said Ms. Frizzle.
"We seem to be blasting off!"

BACK TO SCHOOL?

I'M SO DEPRESSED!

MY PLANETARIUM IS ALWAYS OPEN.

CLOSED FOR REPAIRS

HERE WE GO AGAIN.

NOT ANOTHE CRAZY TRIP!

Far behind, in the black sky,
we saw the planet Earth
getting smaller and smaller.
We were traveling in space!
We had become astronauts!

LOOK HOW SMALL THE EARTH
SEEMS FROM HERE!

CLASS, NOTICE EARTH'S
BLUE OCEANS,
WHITE CLOUDS
AND BROWN LAND.

IT'S BEAUTIFUL!

I THINK, I
HAVE TO GO TO
THE BATHROOM.

The Friz said our first stop
would be the Moon.
We got off the bus and looked around.
There was no air, no water,
no sign of life.
All we saw were dust and rock
and lots and lots of craters.
Ms. Frizzle said the craters were
formed billions of years ago
when the Moon was hit by meteorites.
Meteorites are falling chunks
of rock and metal.

YOUR WEIGHT AND FATE ON THE MOON

lbs.	lbs.
85	14
Earth Weight	Moon Weight

You will travel to far off places.

WE ARE SO LIGHT ON THE MOON!

THAT'S BECAUSE THE MOON HAS LESS GRAVITY THAN THE EARTH.

It was fun on the Moon.
We wanted to play,
but Ms. Frizzle said it was time to go.
So we got back on the bus.
"We'll start with the Sun,
the center of the solar system,"
said the Friz, and we blasted off.

LOOK HOW HIGH WE CAN JUMP!

I WAS IN A NATIONAL JUMP-ROPE CONTEST. I WON, OF COURSE.

IS THERE A NATIONAL BRAGGING CONTEST?

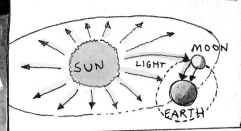

We zoomed toward the Sun,
the biggest, brightest, and hottest
object in the solar system.
Jets of super-hot gases shot out
at us from the surface.
Thank goodness Ms. Frizzle
didn't get *too* close!

She steered around to the other side
and pulled away.
"We'll be seeing all the planets
in order, class," explained Frizzie.
"Mercury is the first planet,
the closest to the Sun."

MY SCHOOL IS HEATED
WITH _SUN_ ENERGY.

I HAVE A _SUN_ DECK.

I HAVE TEN PAIRS
OF _SUNGLASSES_.

GIVE US A
BREAK, JANET.

HOW HOT IS THE SUN?
by Florrie
At the center of
the sun the temper-
ature is about
15 _million_ degrees
Centigrade! The sun
is so hot it heats
planets that are
millions of kilometers
away.

SUN SPOTS
are areas
that are cooler
than the rest
of the Sun.

Our Path So Far

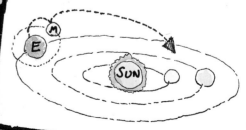

Mercury was a dead, sun-baked planet.
"This planet is a lot like our Moon.
There is no water and hardly any air,"
said the Friz.
"Notice the craters on its surface
as we pass by."

THE SUN LOOKS TWICE AS BIG HERE AS IT DOES FROM EARTH.

THAT'S BECAUSE MERCURY IS SO CLOSE.

TOO CLOSE! LET'S GO!

YOUR WEIGHT AND FATE ON MERCURY

lbs.	lbs.
85	32
Earth Weight	Mercury Weight

You will Vacation in a sunny spot.

Before long, we felt ourselves
being pulled in by the gravity of Venus
—the second planet from the Sun.
Venus was completely covered by
a thick layer of yellowish clouds.
"We will now explore the surface of Venus,"
said Ms. Frizzle.

WHY ARE VENUS'S CLOUDS YELLOW?
by Tim
Earth's clouds are white because they are made of water vapor.
Venus's clouds are made mostly of a deadly yellow poison called <u>sulfuric acid</u>.

WE'RE GAINING WEIGHT, AND WE HAVEN'T EVEN HAD LUNCH.

WE WILL BE HEAVIER HERE THAN ON THE MOON OR MERCURY BECAUSE VENUS HAS MORE GRAVITY.

YOUR WEIGHT AND FATE ON VENUS

lbs. 85 Earth Weight

lbs. 77 Venus weight

Your future looks Cloudy.

SO DOES VENUS!

WHY IS IT SO HOT ON VENUS?
by Ralph
Venus's atmosphere has a lot of carbon dioxide gas in it. Carbon dioxide acts like a blanket to hold heat in.

CLOUDS
HEAT HEAT HEAT

When heat is trapped like this by a planet's atmosphere, it is called the "greenhouse effect."

Below the clouds, Venus was as dry as a desert.
The ground was covered with rocks.
And it was HOT!
It was about 400 degrees Centigrade!
That's *much* hotter than an oven baking cookies!

THERE'S NO LIFE ON VENUS, CLASS.

IT'S TOO HOT!

IT'S TOO DRY!

THERE'S TOO MUCH ACID!

LET'S LEAVE!

The air was so heavy
we could feel it pressing down on us!
Ms. Frizzle said there might be volcanoes
around, too.
We said, "Let's get out of here!"
"Our next stop is Mars,
the red planet, fourth from the Sun,"
announced the Friz.
"On our way, we'll be passing through
the orbit of Earth, the third planet."
The bus lifted off with a roar.

I'VE BEEN TO MARS LOTS OF TIMES.

JUST IGNORE HER.

IT NEVER RAINS ON VENUS
by Dorothy Ann
Venus's clouds never make rain because it is too hot for rain to form. Any liquid on Venus dries up instantly.

Our Path So Far

Looking down, we saw a huge canyon.
Ms. Frizzle said it was
as long as the United States.
There was a volcano
three times taller than
the tallest volcano on Earth.
And all around, there were channels
that looked like dried-up river beds.

Is THERE LIFE ON MARS?
by Molly
No life has been found on Mars. Living things need water, and there is no liquid water on Mars.
So space scientists think life probably cannot exist there!

Polar Ice Cap

Canyon

YOUR WEIGHT AND FATE ON MARS

| lbs. 85 Earth Weight | lbs. 32 Mars Weight |

EARTH IS THE BEST PLANET FOR LIFE. THAT'S WHY I LIVE THERE.

Channels

Things will look rosy soon.

JANET LIKES TO BE THE BEST.

WE NOTICED.

"Mars is the last of what we call
the inner planets!"
Ms. Frizzle shouted above the roar of the rockets.
"We will now be going
through the asteroid belt
to the outer planets!"

THE ASTEROID BELT
by Shirley

The area between the inner and the outer planets is called the asteroid belt. It is filled with thousands and thousands of asteroids.

WHAT ARE ASTEROIDS?
by Florrie

Asteroids are chunks of rock and metal in orbit around the Sun.

Scientists think they are the building blocks of a planet that never formed.

Thousands of asteroids were spinning all around us.
All at once, we heard
the tinkling of broken glass.
One of our taillights
had been hit by an asteroid.
Ms. Frizzle put the bus on autopilot
and went out to take a look.
She kept on talking about asteroids
over the bus radio.

THE LARGEST ASTEROID IS ONLY ⅓ THE SIZE OF OUR MOON. MOST ASTEROIDS ARE THE SIZE OF HOUSES OR SMALLER.

I WISH SHE'D COME INSIDE.

Suddenly there was a snap.
Ms. Frizzle's tether line had broken!
Without warning,
the rockets fired up,
and the bus zoomed away!
The autopilot was malfunctioning.

On the radio, Ms. Frizzle's voice grew fainter and fainter.
Then she was gone.
We were on our own!
We were lost in the solar system!

Most of us were too scared to move.
But Janet started searching the bus.
In the glove compartment
she found Ms. Frizzle's lesson book.
As she began reading from it,
a huge planet came into view.
"Class, this is Jupiter," Janet read.
"It's the first of the outer planets,
and the largest planet in the solar system."

WHAT ARE SATURN'S RINGS?
by Rachel

Saturn's rings are made of ice, rock and dust — all in orbit around the planet.

The next sight made us forget our troubles.
It was Saturn, a gas planet like Jupiter.
It had swirling clouds and lots of moons.
But the most incredible thing about Saturn
was its rings.
It was the most beautiful planet
in the solar system!

YOUR WEIGHT AND FATE ON SATURN

lbs.	lbs.
85	90
Earth Weight	Saturn Weight

There's a ring in your future.

"There are thousands of rings around Saturn, class."

THEY LOOK LIKE THE GROOVES IN A PHONOGRAPH RECORD.

SATURN IS THE GROOVIEST PLANET, MAN!

The bus was going faster and faster,
and we couldn't control the autopilot.
We swept past stormy Neptune,
another blue-green planet—eighth from the Sun.
All we could think about
was finding Ms. Frizzle!

"Neptune
is the last
of the giant
gas planets."

WE'RE ALMOST
OUT OF GAS
OURSELVES!

Great Dark Spot

AND THE NEAREST
SERVICE STATION
IS 4,000 MILLION
KILOMETERS AWAY.

o HOW LONG IS A YEAR?
by Tim
A year is the time
it takes for a planet
to go all around the
sun. Neptune and
o Uranus are so far away
from the sun that
they have very long
years.
o One year on Uranus is
84 Earth years.

Neptune's year is
o 165 Earth years.

YOUR WEIGHT AND FATE
ON NEPTUNE

lbs.	lbs.
85	97
Earth Weight	Neptune Weight

You will have a
happy birthday
165 years from now.

IS PLUTO A REAL PLANET?
by Wanda
Some scientists think Pluto was once a moon of Neptune. It may have escaped from the orbit around Neptune. Then it became a real planet in orbit around the Sun. Pluto was the last planet discovered in the known Solar system.

YOUR WEIGHT AND FATE ON PLUTO

| lbs. 85 Earth Weight | lbs. 1½ Pluto Weight |

You will meet a small, dark planet.

CHARON

PLUTO

We were going so fast,
we almost missed seeing the ninth planet,
tiny Pluto,* and its moon, Charon.
We were so far away from the Sun that it
didn't look big anymore.
It just looked like a very bright star.
We were leaving the solar system.

*Every 248 years, Neptune's orbit is further out than Pluto's. Then Neptune is the ninth planet. But most of the time, Pluto is the ninth planet from the Sun.

THERE'S NOTHING OUT THERE— BUT STARS.

MAYBE THERE'S A TENTH PLANET WAITING TO BE DISCOVERED.

IT'LL HAVE TO WAIT.

I HOPE MS. FRIZZLE IS WAITING, TOO.

Janet flipped rapidly
through Ms. Frizzle's book.
Suddenly she found something new—
the instructions for the autopilot.
We punched in ASTEROID BELT
on the control panel.
Slowly the bus turned around.
It was working! We were going back!

ASTEROID BELT **

Auto-Pilot

JANET REALLY SAVED THE DAY.

I TOLD YOU SHE'S A GOOD KID.

Our Path so far

E M S M V M J S U N P

Asteroid Belt

With Frizzie back at the wheel,
the bus headed straight for Earth.
We reentered the atmosphere,
landed with a thump,
and looked around.

BOYS AND GIRLS,
WE ARE ARRIVING
ON EARTH, THE
THIRD PLANET
FROM THE SUN.

THUMP

We were in the school parking lot again.
The rockets were gone.
The space suits were gone.
The bus was a wreck.
Everything was back to normal.

THANK GOODNESS!

HELLO AGAIN,
OLD FRIEND.

OUR PLANET CHART

PLANET	HOW BIG ACROSS	HOW LONG ONE ROTATION (DAY AND NIGHT)	HOW LONG ONE YEAR	HOW FAR FROM THE SUN	HOW MANY MOONS	HOW MANY RINGS
MERCURY	4,900 km.	59 days	88 days	57.9 million km.	None	None
VENUS	12,100 km.	243 days	224.7 days	108.2 million km.	None	None
EARTH	12,756 km.	24 hours	365.3 days	149.6 million Km.	1 5 1	None
MARS	6,800 Km.	24.5 hours	687 days	227.8 million Km.	1 2 2 2	None
JUPITER	142,800 Km.	9.8 hours	12 Earth Years	778 million Km.	at least 16	2
SATURN	120,660 km.	10.7 hours	29.5 Earth Years	1,427 million Km.	at least 17	Many
URANUS	52,400 km.	17 hours	84 Earth Years	2,870 million Km.	at least 15	10
NEPTUNE	49,500 Km.	16 hours	165 Earth Years	4,500 million Km.	8	4
PLUTO	about 2,300 km.	6 days	248 Earth years	5,900 million Km.	1	None

In the classroom,
we made a terrific
chart of the planets
and a mobile of the solar system.

At last, it was time to go home.
It had been a typical day
in Ms. Frizzle's class.
Now we had only one problem.
Would anyone ever believe us
when we told about our trip?

ATTENTION, READERS!

DO NOT ATTEMPT THIS TRIP ON YOUR OWN SCHOOL BUS!

Three reasons why not:

1. Attaching rockets to your school bus will upset your teacher, the school principal, and your parents. It will not get you into orbit anyway. An ordinary bus cannot travel in outer space, and you cannot become astronauts without years of training.

2. Landing on certain planets may be dangerous to your health. Even astronauts cannot visit Venus (it's too hot), Mercury (it's too close to the Sun), or Jupiter (its gravity would crush human beings). People cannot fly to the Sun, either. Its gravity and heat would be too strong.

3. Space travel could make you miss dinner with your family... for the rest of your childhood. Even if a school bus could go to outer space, it could never travel through the entire solar system in one day. It took years for the Voyager space probes to do that.

ON THE OTHER HAND...

If a red-haired teacher in a funny dress shows up at your school — start packing!